Class 9 and The Monsters From Under the Sea

by

Mark Baker

Also by Mark Baker

For kids:

"Class 9 and the Monsters from Out of Space"

"Full of adventure, fun and laughs. Delights and imaginative storytelling on every page." (Kay)

"Really fun to read and it made me feel I wanted to be part of Class 9!" (Margaret)

For adults:

"Biscuits: A comedy and an adventure"

"Very funny. Loads of great ideas. Lots of laugh out loud moments." (Frank)

"Wonderfully odd, imaginative and intriguing." (Caroline)

Class 9 and

The Monsters

From

Under the Sea

by Mark Baker

Cover Illustration: Florence Davis

Chapter 1. The school trip.

"Wheeeeee!!" went Sidney Brown. "Wheeeeeeee!!!" The boy ran about the playground pretending to be an aeroplane.

"What's up with him?" asked Sandra, Pinkerton Primary School's cleaner.

"He's excited," said Sharon, Sidney's mum.

"Why?"

"They've got a trip."

"Oh, yes, I'd forgotten," said Sandra. "Is that today?"

"Yes it is. It's why we're here early. The Year 4 trip to Colwyn Bay."

"Nice! I like it there!"

"Never been."

"You should. It's gorgeous!"

"Wheeeee!!!" Sidney went. He whirled round and round. It was half past seven in the morning.

"Where do they get the energy from?" asked Sharon.

"Search me!" replied the cleaner.

The rest of Class 9 arrived in dribs and drabs over the next twenty minutes or so and by eight o'clock they were all present. At eight o'clock on the dot, the school clock chimed then Mr Parsnip, Class 9's teacher, emerged from inside the school.

"Good morning everyone!" he cried. He was always cheerful, Mr P, and today was no exception. He was very much looking forward to their holiday.

"How are we all today?" he asked.

Loads of the kids cheered in reply to this and the parents looked pretty pleased too. They were glad they were going to get rid of their children for a few days. Get some peace and quiet. They did not envy Mr Parsnip nor Miss Beetroot or Mrs Pear who would be looking after the kids day and night for the duration of the trip. "Huh!" some thought, "Mr Parsnip is looking all right now – wait til we see him when they return! He'll be a total wreck then!!"

The parents didn't know though that Mr Parsnip was in fact an intergalactic traveller who had been sent by the Space Council to Pinkerton to look after Class 9 and to guard the portal to other worlds that lay in the corner of the staff room.

He did his best to conceal this fact. His space suits were hidden in an old suitcase in his loft. His rocket boots were in a cardboard box in the garag

old newspapers. His laser gun was in the

He'd forgotten all about that for the

concentrate on teaching Class 9. Maths, English,

– that kind of thing. It was relaxing, far more relaxing than fighting the Boogles with their fifteen heads and five hundred razor sharp claws, which was what he had been doing when he'd got the call to come to Earth, to Pinkerton Primary School, to Class 9.

Yep, it was going to be a lovely, fun, relaxing week on the coast with a cool bunch of kids like Keith, Honey, Anish, Nancy and Bob. He couldn't wait to begin.

"Line up over here," he said to the kids. The kids gave their parents a final hug then got in a line. Mr Parsnip saw them into the coach.

"This is so exciting!" said Nedrun to Tina as they grabbed a pair of cool seats near the back of the coach.

"I know, right?" Tina replied.

The two girls turned to look out of the window at the parents who had moved onto the pavement so they could wave goodbye to them.

"We are going to have an AMAZING time!" reckoned Sudric.

“Yesssss!” agreed Del. It was the moment they’d been waiting for all their lives.

“Bye, Mum!” cried Dizzy.

“Bye!” shouted Jeffrey as the enormous coach wheeled away, into the road, off towards Colwyn Bay.

“I hope they’ll be all right,” said Sharon. It was the first time Sidney had been on holiday without her.

“They’ll be fine,” replied May, Arnold Steenburgen’s mum. “It’s only a school trip. What could possibly happen?”

“I suppose you’re right.”

“Of course I am. Come on, come and get a cup of coffee.”

“Ooh, all right then.”

The coach picked up speed and headed out of the small village of Pinkerton onto the open roads. The children settled down to enjoy the journey, some of them reading, others chatting with their mates, a few of them simply gazing out of the window at the sights that flashed past.

Meanwhile, the monsters who were under the sea said, “blub, blub!”

Chapter 2. Colwyn Bay.

It was a long journey. When they got there, it was tea-time. Time to take their suitcases off the coach, find out where their rooms were and then come down to the dining hall for food.

The man in charge of the place introduced himself. “Hello, there, my name is Ronald Fish. Ha ha, yes, that’s quite funny because we live by the sea and there are lots of fish in there!!” Ronald Fish laughed but no-one else did. Well, Eric did but then he laughed at most things.

“He’s a weird one,” thought Vanessa and Fish did look strange. He looked like a fish in fact with very pale skin through which you could see his veins, wet-looking hair and when he finished talking, he kept opening and closing his mouth like a fish. Crazy!!

Another adult brought out the dinner – sausages and mash. This was a great favourite of Class 9’s and there were huge steaming platefuls. Trinny and Timmy were the first to be served and they tucked in straight away. They both sighed, “mmmmmm!” as the delicious nosh passed their taste buds and before long the whole room was filled with similar sounds from everyone.

Mr Parsnip enjoyed his sausages and mash too. As he ate, he looked out through the window onto the beach and ran through in his mind the plan for the rest of the day. After their meal, they'd go for a walk along the beach towards the pier and have a game of football on the sand. Then they'd stop off at a café for hot chocolate before returning to the house, getting unpacked and going to bed.

Sounded good. Everything was going according to plan so far. They were a great bunch of kids who deserved a holiday. They'd been working hard at their Maths and English but much more than that, a few weeks earlier, they had endured a very trying experience.

Earth had been invaded by monsters and Class 9 had defeated them. It had been very difficult but also they'd had to keep it secret from everyone else. So they didn't get any credit for what they'd done – in fact, they got into a whole load of trouble with their parents and Mr Loaf the headteacher.

It was really unfair. Mr Parsnip knew all about it though so he was determined to give them the best time he could to reward them for saving the whole darned world. Cos that kind of thing ain't easy, ya know!

The kids finished their tea then everyone headed out to the beach. It was starting to get chilly so they did up their coats and trudged on to the sand. Colwyn Bay – they'd studied about it in Geography – seen videos, read articles, and now they were here and they thought it was lovely. Soft, golden sand, rolling waves and best of all, no-one else around. It was a little bit early in the year really for a school trip so that was probably why.

The children walked along the beach enjoying the feeling of the sand beneath their feet. Some of them chatted boisterously in groups; others strolled alone and gazed at the Big Blue; a few dashed and sprinted, fell over and got up again. It wasn't long before they arrived at the pier.

The pier was old and broken. And closed. The council had shut it a few years back because there was no money to fix it. It was a ruin sitting there partly on the land and partly in the sea.

"We should go onto it!" cried Trinny.

"It's too dangerous," replied Mr Parsnip. "Look," he said and he pointed to a sign that read,

DANGER!!

DO NOT ENTER!!!

“Come on, Mr P!” said Eddie. “We’re Class 9. We can do anything!”

“Sorry,” said Mr P. “One of us might fall through the rotten wood and hurt ourselves.”

“Someone’s in there!” said Arnold.

“What!?” asked Mr P.

“I definitely saw something move in there, something white.”

The gang stopped still for a while to gaze at the pier and see if they could back up what Arnold had said. But whoever it was – if it had been anyone – had gone.

“Come on then!” cried Keith. “Time for football!” And with that, everyone forgot about the pier. Mr Parsnip took out the ball from his rucksack, threw it onto the sand and watched the kids descend on it like sharks onto nice juicy fish.

Mr Parsnip set out some goals. “All right!” he cried. “West Ham supporters against the rest!” This got everyone excited – the kids were very passionate about their choice of football team – and they loved to express support for their side and dislike of any other.

"Boooo!" shouted Dizzy when she heard the words, "West Ham." She loved Tottenham so she went on the same team as Rudolph who supported Arsenal and Leloo who liked Liverpool.

They went up by the pier and turned around to face the West Ham supporters. A few kids sat out to watch or chat with their mates. Some went for a walk down towards the sea.

It was a fabulous game. Everyone threw themselves into it. But everybody fell over A LOT because they were playing on sand! It didn't matter though – you just got a bit sandy and then picked yourself up again.

In the end, West Ham won 15-14. At least, that's what Mr Parsnip said. Dizzy told him he was cheating and that her team had won 17-12.

"You can't count that high!" joked Mr Parsnip.

"That's because you're such a bad Maths teacher!" Dizzy replied, laughing.

"You ungrateful child!" he protested.

"Yeah, well, here's a present for you," she shouted and she threw a piece of seaweed at him.

"Right, that's it!" he cried. "You're in big trouble now!" He bent down to pick up his own piece of seaweed and Dizzy screamed and wheeled away across the sand. While he was doing that, Tyke joined in and landed his own piece of seaweed flat bang on the back of Mr Parsnip's head.

"Hey!" the teacher cried. Ewww, it was wet and slimy, not very nice at all and it looked like it might be him against the whole of Class 9 at this rate. He didn't like those odds.

"Who's with me?" Parsnip shouted.

"I am!" said Trinny.

"And me!" Nancy yelled.

In the end a whole bunch of kids joined the teacher while Mrs Pear went with the others. They raced around throwing seaweed at each other whilst shrieking and screaming and having a fabulous time. Golly, this was fun!

The gang sat down afterwards on the beach and drank hot chocolate from thermos flasks Miss Beetroot had brought along. There were lovely homemade cookies too.

"This is the best day ever," said Su.

"Yep," replied Tina. "The best day ever."

Chapter 3. Night.

It was a bunch of weary children who returned to the hostel. They'd worn themselves out. It was all most of them could do to take their toothbrushes from their wash bags, clean their teeth, wash their faces and get undressed before tumbling into bed and under the covers. Most of them were asleep within moments, straight into the dreamland that less and less these days was made up of Rinky-Dinkies and more and more consisted of pleasanter things. Tonight, maybe they would dream of beach football and hot chocolate.

The adults looked in on them a while later and were pleased to see they were all asleep. "Right!" said Mr Parsnip. "Let's have a cup of tea and then we can discuss what's going on tomorrow." He went off to make a brew while the ladies went into the lounge.

"I'm exhausted already!" said Miss Beetroot.

"Me too!" replied Mrs Pear.

Mr Parsnip returned with three cups of tea and a few biscuits. "Now," he said, "tomorrow, we are going to the Welsh Mountain Zoo, a conservation zoo with rare animals like red pandas, tigers and snow leopards."

"That sounds amazing!" said Miss Beetroot.

"I know!" replied Mr P. "I reckon the kids will love it!"

"We're having a picnic at lunchtime?" asked Mrs Pear.

"That's right and then we'll come back here for supper."

"Brilliant!" said Mrs Pear. "Anyway, I think I'm going to take my cup of tea to bed. I'm very tired and I need to get my strength up for the zoo!"

"Good idea, Daphne," said Mr P. "We won't be far behind."

Mr Parsnip and Miss Beetroot chatted for a while then they went to bed as well, though not before checking on the children one last time. "They're a good bunch, aren't they, Rosemary?" Mr Parsnip observed.

"They certainly are, Jeremy," his TA agreed.

Then they went to bed and the whole place became quiet.

Then the monsters came.

They came from underneath the sea. "Blub blub," they moaned as they crawled from their watery lair.

“Blub blub,” they groaned as they sploshed over the beach towards the hostel where the children were asleep. “Blub blub blub,” they screeched as they arrived at the hostel. The creatures surrounded it. Some of them looked in through the windows. Another one pushed against the front door. It was open! Ronald Fish had left it open! The first monster pushed his way into the house. He went into the hall, looked around and decided he would go up the stairs. Up he went, gliding over them, making only quiet, squelchy sounds.

Behind him, the rest of the monsters filed into the house. Each one of them stood in the hall for a moment before deciding where to go. Some of them also went upstairs, others went towards the dining hall and kitchen. Some opened the doors of the rooms downstairs.

Nedrun was sleeping very well. It was the first time she’d been away from her family. She’d been a bit nervous beforehand but now they’d arrived it was everything she could have hoped for. And more. Class 9 were so great – she knew she was going to have a fantastic time with her friends.

She was having a dream about red pandas – playing with them in the sand. There were lots of them and they were a bit naughty but so-o cute. She loved to hold them and stroke them and play games with them. Then one of them put his paw on her face and it was wet. Urggghhh! she went. That wasn't very nice. Then it did it again and it was really really wet this time. Ewwwww!! It was so wet that she woke up and saw a monster sitting on top of her.

"Waaaaahhhhh!" she cried at the top of her pretty loud voice. She gave the creature a big push off of her and moved her body at a million miles an hour away from the beast out of the other side of the bed and onto the ground. "Ouch!" she moaned – she'd banged her elbow - but there was no time to think about that. The creature was coming round the end of the bed and heading for her again.

"Right!" Nedrun said, and she summoned up all of her bravery and as the monster closed in, she leapt onto the bed, one step and then over it, past the beast and out through the door into the hall.

Where she saw ten more beasts. "Waaaaaahhhh!!" she cried again. This was a bit much. They were supposed to be here on holiday, having a nice time, not fighting monsters again!

All ten of them turned round to look at her.

The creatures were white, with black eyes that poked out from underneath their hair which went right down to the ground. They were the shape of a little hill and overall they looked like … mops. Yes, thought Nedrun, that was it, they were mops. Without the handles. She would have laughed if she hadn't been so scared.

The monsters were working as a team, not leaving any gaps between them. Nedrun was trapped. They were going to get her!

Then Keith came out of his room carrying a broomstick. "Rarrrrrr!" he went, ultra-fierce and started hitting the nearest mop to him with the stick. "Blub!" cried the mop in a high-pitched voice. It turned around to find out who was hitting it and Keith got in a couple more blows.

Nedrun suddenly realised she was standing next to a floor lamp. She bent down, quick as a flash unplugged it, then picked it up and wielded it like a light saber. The left hand side she smashed into one of the mops and sent it tumbling, then the right went into another and pushed that one back as well.

"Brilliant!" she thought. "I reckon we stand a chance now, me and Keith against eleven monsters. After all, they don't seem to be fast. Or big. Or strong! If I just stand here and swing the lamp, I should be able to fight them off."

So that is what she did, though she only had to do it for a couple of seconds cos after that, the thing that ought to have happened ages ago (and in the back of her mind she'd been wondering why it hadn't happened) happened.

Everyone else woke up.

Sidney steamed out of his room with a tennis racket and started beating one of the mops. Sudric jumped right on top of another mop and tried to wrestle it to the ground. Honey Barber tried out some of her kickboxing moves on another. Before long the house was full of children and mops fighting.

Ronald Fish came out of his room dressed in fishy-patterned pyjamas and squeaked like a fish when he saw what was going on. "Waaaaaah!" he wailed. His room was near the front door which for the moment was unguarded so he took the opportunity and headed out of it and into the night, probably never to be seen again.

Mr Parsnip, Miss Beetroot and Mrs Pear came out of their rooms as well. "This exact thing happened on Proxima Centauri b!" he thought to himself. He wished he had his laser gun with him but he'd left it at home. All he did have was a packet of biscuits that he kept by his bed to snack on if he woke up in the night. So he picked those up and started throwing them at the nearest mop.

All of this carried on for a while. The mops and the children were evenly matched. The mops were actually not very ferocious. They didn't have sharp claws or teeth or anything like that. If they got a hold of you, all they seemed to do was squelch and splodge you. Three of them cornered Jeffrey. They took it in turns to go up to him and rub their wet bodies all over him. Ewwww, thought Jeff, it was rather cold, and salty, but not too bad to be honest. It was just water after all.

So it continued for a while and actually everyone started to have quite a good time. It was quite good fun fighting the mops. It might have continued all night if Arnold Steenburgen hadn't suddenly emerged from his room and shouted "Stop!" at the top of his voice.

He was usually a quiet lad in class, so this shouting came as a surprise. It was so loud!! "Stop!" he yelled and everyone stopped. The children, the adults, the mops.

"What are you doing?" he asked.

It seemed like an odd question. Wasn't it obvious what they were doing? What were they supposed to be doing?

"We're fighting these mops," replied Kay eventually.

"Why?" Arnold asked.

"Why!?" repeated Kay. "Because they're attacking us!"

"No they're not," said Arnold.

"No?"

"NO!!!" he cried. He went on to explain that he had been for the last ten minutes in his room talking to one of the monsters.

"But all they can say is 'blub'," protested Nedrun.

"All you say is 'blah blah blah'," countered Arnold, "but I don't complain about it!"

"Oi!" said Nedrun. "That's cheeky!"

"I know, right?" replied Arnold forcefully, which took Nedrun right aback and allowed him to continue. "These creatures have not come here to attack us; they've come to be our friends!"

"Are you sure about that, Arnold?" Mr Parsnip asked him.

"Yes! Of course! Look, has any of them actually hurt anyone?"

Everybody looked around at each other to see if anyone had been hurt. And it didn't seem that they had.

"I was splodged!" protested Jeffrey.

"They're simply being friendly," said Arnold.

"Well, I didn't like it very much," said Jeff.

"Blub blub blub, blub blub blub!" said Arnold quite sharply to the three mops surrounding Jeff.

They squealed, "blub blub blub" in a very pathetic, high-pitched way, then fell onto their sides and rolled around still squealing.

"That's them saying 'sorry'," Arnold said.

"How do you know all this?" asked Mr Parsnip, incredulous.

"They told me," Arnold said.

It seemed that Arnold could understand the sea creatures. Apparently, they had told him that they had lived at Colwyn Bay under the sea for two hundred years.

It was quite nice under there but a bit wet. Sometimes they would come on to the beach and play for a while but only when there weren't any people around because they were so shy.

When they had heard and seen Class 9 playing on the beach earlier though, the mops had been amazed by how lovely and fun the children were. They'd had a meeting and decided they would go and introduce themselves to the children and see if they could become friends.

And that is what they had done.

"They scared the life out of me!" protested Nedrun.

"Me too!" complained Keith.

"Well, they're very sorry," said Arnold Steenburgen. "They didn't mean to, and they'd like to be friends. If we would."

The kids of Class 9 looked at the monsters. This was weird, monsters who weren't evil, monsters who didn't want to eat you. Hmmmmm, and they were kind of cute. A bit like strange dogs. It could be fun.

"What do you think, Mr P?" Nancy asked.

"It's up to you!" he said.

"Then I vote, 'YAYYYYYY!!'"

"Me too!" shouted Bob.

“And me!” yelled Peter.

“YAYYYYY!!” cried everyone. It was decided. The mops were here to stay.

Chapter 4. The next day.

The next day, they were supposed to have been going to the zoo but the kids all got together and persuaded Mr P that they didn't want to do that. Maybe later in the week. They just wanted to play with the mops.

So after breakfast, everyone went down to the beach and waited. And they waited. And then after about fifteen minutes, the mops came out of the sea. It was so cool! If they hadn't known the mops were friendly, they'd've been frightened to death but as it was they were overjoyed. "Yayyyyy!" everybody cried.

There were about 100 mops and 30 children, so each child had plenty of Plinky-Plonkies (Arnold told the class this was what the mops' real name.)

"Plinky-Plonky?" questioned Eddie. "Sounds a bit like 'Rinky-Dinky'!"

"They're very different to the Rinky-Dinkies!" Arnold scolded him.

"Whatever. We'll see," said Ed and during the morning they did see that the Plinky-Plonkies were in fact very sweet and fun. They were similar to dogs. The first thing the kids did with them was throw some sticks and the Plinky-Plonkies loved fetching them.

The PPs were big enough for the kids to clamber on top of and once they'd got the hang of that, they had races across the sand. The creatures were fast and once they got above a certain speed, the children flew off. It was really hard to hold on to the mops because they were so wet!

The kids, Mr Baker and the two TAs had lunch while the mops disappeared back under the waves to eat their food.

"What do they eat, Arnold?" Sudric asked.

"Fish," he replied. "Obviously."

"I see."

The rest of the week went by swimmingly. The class had a few outings to local tourist spots, including the zoo, but always came back early so they could play with the mops.

Then, before they knew it, the week was over. It was time to go home. "Come on, everyone!" said Mr P. "Pack up all your stuff and let's head back to Pinkerton. Your parents will be missing you."

"Ah, no!" said Ricky.

“I’m afraid so, Ricky,” said Mr Parsnip. “All good things have to come to an end.”

The children went and packed all their stuff. It took them about half an hour. Then they got on the coach. Mr Parsnip counted them as they climbed on board. “One … two … three …” he said. Nancy, Kay and Nedrun were the first ones on. They shot to the back of the bus.

“Fifteen … sixteen … seventeen …” Rudolph, Derek and Eric boarded the coach. The queue of kids dwindled and dwindled until there were only two left at the back of the line – Charmaine, and, last of all, Dizzy. “Twenty-eight … twenty-nine …” went Mr Parsnip. “Hold on, I must have made a mistake. There should be thirty children.” He got onto the coach and counted the children again. And then he counted them again. And then again, just to make sure. There was only 29. One child was missing.

“Who is it?” asked Mr Parsnip. “Who is missing?”

“Put up your hand if you’re missing!” snorted Eric. He thought it was funny. No-one else did.

The children tried to work out who it was wasn’t there. They all got it at the same time, “It’s Arnold!” they cried.

Arnold! Mr Parsnip and Mrs Pear went into the house and called out "Arnold! Come on now!" There was no reply. They went onto the beach and looked around but he was nowhere.

"Let's look in his room," suggested Mrs Pear.

"Ok," agreed Parsnip so they climbed the stairs to the room where Arnold had been staying these last few days, where he'd first met and talked to the mop. His rucksack was lying on the bed. His clothes were still in the wardrobe. And there was a little note on his bedside table which read:

Dear Mr Parsnip and Class 9,

I have gone to live underwater with the Plinky-Plonkies.

Goodbye

Arnold Steenburgen.

A brief piece of writing as always from Arnold. Though this one had considerably more impact than most of the stories he wrote during English lesson. Mr Parsnip raised his head and yelled, "Waaaaaaahhhhhh!"

Chapter 5. A submarine.

This one would be hard to explain to Arnold's parents. "Excuse me, Mr and Mrs Steenburgen. I'm sorry, we haven't been able to bring Arnold back with us from the school trip cos he'd decided he wants to live underwater with monsters!"

Hmmm, yes, that probably wouldn't go down well with the parents. Or with the headteacher, come to that. Or with anyone. Arnold Steenburgen had gone to live underwater with the mops. Right! Something needed to be done.

First, Parsnip went out to the coach to tell them what had happened.

"Cool!" said Ralph.

"It is not cool!" replied Mr Parsnip. "It is insane!! He can't live underwater with the mops. We will have to go and get him."

"Ooh!" thought Class 9. "This sounds like an expedition! An adventure maybe." They'd enjoyed the holiday but it hadn't been very dangerous. After their encounter with the Rinky-Dinkies, they'd developed a taste for thrills and spills.

Honey Barber raised an interesting point. “How is he breathing underwater?”

“I don’t know, Honey. How did he manage to speak to the Mops? It seems there is more to Arnold than we previously thought.”

“Hmmm,” thought Honey. “Breathing underwater. That could be useful. I wonder if Arnold could teach me how to do that!”

“How are we going to get him?” asked Tim. Another good question.

“Well,” said Mr P. “As it happens, I have a submarine which I use from time to time. At the moment, it’s moored off Widow’s Peak. Fortunately I have a remote control so I can get it here pretty fast.”

Mr Parsnip took from his pocket a remote control with lots of dials and buttons on it. He turned some of the dials, pressed a couple of the buttons, murmured, “That should do it!”, then put it away again. “The submarine will be here in thirty minutes!” he announced.

“Great!” everyone cried. “Just time for another game of football!” The kids piled off the coach, grabbed a ball and started playing on the sand.

Mr Parsnip went into the house and got a sharp knife. He then used it to slash one of the tyres of the coach. “What are you doing?” asked the coach driver. “Have you gone mad?”

“Sorry, old chap,” replied P. “I’m not a liar,” he added, mysteriously.

“What does that mean?” asked the driver but Parsnip was already on the phone to the school.

“Hello?” said P. “Is that Mr Loaf? Hello, it’s Mr Parsnip here.

“Oh hello, Parsnip. How are you? Have you had a good week?” replied the headteacher.

“Yes, lovely, thanks. We’ve got a slight problem though. We were about to set off for home and the coach tyre has been slashed. So we’ll need to get the AA out to repair it. I’m afraid that might delay us a while.”

“Oh well, not to worry,” said Loaf. “I’ll let the parents know you’re going to be a little bit late.”

“Thanks” said P and hung up.

The coach driver had been watching and listening to this. “See?” said Mr P. “I’m not allowed to lie. As a teacher, it’s against the rules. If it was found out I’d lied I’d get fired straightaway.”

"But you're allowed to slash the tyres of my coach, are you?" enquired the coach driver grumpily.

"Yes I am," said P. "There's nothing in the rules about that!"

The kids played football while Mr Parsnip waited by the water. There were no mops to be seen. Hmmm, he thought, haven't got the nerve to show their faces! Ooh, he'd give them a talking to when he got a hold of them!

After twenty-nine minutes and thirty-five seconds, there was a disturbance in the water in front of him. And then suddenly, a sleek, yellow submarine came to the surface. It sprouted wheels and trundled up to him on the sand.

The children froze in the middle of their game. Even Bob for whom football was more important than life itself, instantly, entirely forgot about the ball they were kicking and stopped to gaze at the magnificent machine. And then after the surprise it was a race to see who could get there first. It was a race, as usual, between Honey and Rudolph. The two of them sprinted through the sand totally determined to prevail. In the end, they both laid their hands on the submarine at the same time.

“Whaddaya think, kids?” Mr Parsnip asked proudly.

“Wow! It’s amazing!” said everyone. Everyone had caught up with Honey and Rudolph by this time. They had spread out around the submarine to take a good look at it.

It looked like an aeroplane without wings was Dizzy’s opinion. There were lots of little windows the children would be able to look out of as they travelled along. It was shiny, it was big and it was yellow.

“Why is it yellow?” Eric asked.

“Why is it yellow?!” repeated Mr Parsnip. “Don’t you guys know anything? Who is your teacher? I must have stern words with him.”

“Nope. Still don’t get it,” said Mark.

Mr Parsnip took his phone out of his pocket, got youtube up, then typed in “Yellow Submarine”.

“Oh, the Beatles!” cried Tim. He’d heard about loads of stuff like that. Quite a few of them had heard of the Beatles though even though they’d been around ages ago.

Mr Parsnip began to play the video. It was this really cool cartoon about a bunch of musicians who went to live under the sea in a yellow submarine.

"Yayyyy!" cried Su. "That's gonna be us!" And indeed it was. Mr Parsnip opened the door and everyone piled in. There was plenty of room for everyone. He counted them on – still 29. Only one child missing – Arnold S.

"Are you coming, ladies?" Mr Parsnip asked the two TAs.

"Yes, please!" they said. "We wouldn't miss this for the world." Mrs Pear and Miss Beetroot got on, found a seat and then Mr Parsnip closed the door behind.

"Everyone ready!?" he cried.

"Yayyyy!" the gang replied. And under the sea they went. They sang,

We all live in a yellow submarine,
Yellow submarine, yellow submarine,
We all live in a yellow submarine,
Yellow submarine, yellow submarine.

Chapter 6. Under the sea.

It was cool down there. Just the very idea of being in a submarine underwater was amazingly cool. None of their mates back at school, none of their brothers or sisters would ever have done this, that was guaranteed.

To start with, it was mainly just water. A few fish here and there. Whenever they saw one though it was really exciting. One orange-coloured one swam right up to the submarine and looked in.

"Hello, fishy!" Eric cried.

"I don't think it can hear you," Jeffrey observed.

"You never know!" said E.

It was true. You never did know these days. It seemed that anything was possible! Maybe the fish had heard Eric speak and it was heading back to its secret underwater headquarters to make a report.

"Hello, Captain!" it might say.

"Yes, what is it, Fish number 2?"

"There's a yellow submarine over there."

"Ooh, well, that'll either be the Beatles or Mr Parsnip. How exciting! Something is happening!!"

That was probably what was going on, Eric reckoned. Jeffrey, on the other hand, thought it was just a normal, ordinary fish who had no idea who they were. Who was right? There was no way of telling. They couldn't turn the submarine around to follow the fish. They had a much more urgent mission to fulfil. Find Arnold Steenburgen.

"How are we going to find him?" Vanessa asked Mr P.

"There's a sonar," replied the teacher. "It can detect human life forms. Fortunately for us, and apart from us, there are not many humans down here."

"How many are there?"

"One."

"Arnold!"

"I hope so."

"Where is he?"

"Right there," said Mr P and he pointed to a screen. There was a picture of the ocean, a picture of their submarine and on the other side of the screen, a blinking red dot.

"The dot is Arnold?"

"Indeed!"

"How far away is that?"

"About five miles," said Mr P. "He's at the bottom of the sea. Listen up, everyone, fasten your seatbelts! We're going down deep!"

And indeed they were. They had been travelling along quite pleasantly and gently until that point but suddenly the submarine plunged downwards.

"Whoa!" cried Tyke.

"Aaaaaahh!" wailed Nancy.

"Hold onnnn!" shouted Mrs Pear.

Down the submarine went, down and down. The further it went the weirder the fish got. One of them looked like a giant balloon that was transparent so you could see its insides. Another one was quite small but had a massive mouth with dozens of sharp teeth and a very fierce expression on its face. Still another was a luminous green and blue colour – very pretty indeed. There was loads to look at for the children. They were silent as mice, not wanting to miss a thing.

Apart from the fish, there was just the sea. The big blue ocean that went on for miles and miles. Until they saw something dark beneath them, getting bigger as they approached.

"What's that?" asked Ricky.

"I don't know," replied Ralph. But as the dark thing grew larger and larger, they could see it was rock and as they got even nearer they could see that carved into the rock was a cave.

"Arnold must be in there!" cried Ricky and indeed, that was where the submarine was going. As it approached the cave, it slowed right down, enabling the children to take a good look at the rock. It was black but also sparkly as if there were tiny crystals embedded inside. It was beautiful *and* scary.

The submarine kept going down but very slowly now and as it did, a great big darkness opened up in front of them.

Mr Parsnip stopped the submarine there for a moment so that he could come back and talk to everyone. "All right, guys?" he asked them to start with.

"Yesss!" everyone replied, their faces shining with excitement. It was nice to have their teacher with them on this adventure. They'd had to do the last one on their own.

"Arnold is inside this cave. We're going to go in. Now, no-one knows what might be in there. It could well be very dangerous. If anyone wants to go back, I understand. There's a little escape pod – Miss Beetroot will take anyone who wants to, back to land. Anyone?"

The children looked round at each other. Was anyone going to put their hand up? Who was gonna be a chicken? No-one! Nobody put their hand up.

"Everyone wants to stay, is that right?" Mr Parsnip asked them again.

"Yessss!" cried all of the children. "Let's go!!"

"All right!" said Mr Parsnip. He returned to the front of the submarine for the delicate task of guiding it into the cave.

They had to go very very slowly through there – they did not want to bash into the walls of the cave. After a while, they were surrounded on both sides by the sparkly black rock. Ahead of them the dark.

"This is scary!" shivered Tina.

"I know, right?" replied Su.

On they went. What would they find at the end of it all? Could Arnold really be all the way down here? How on earth had he managed to get here!?

After a while the darkness in front of them lightened a bit. It wasn't quite as black. As they edged forward, it turned into a glow. Light! There was light up ahead!

"Look at that!" everyone cried. "We must be getting close!" And indeed they were. The glow got brighter and brighter until the submarine turned a corner and there it was

The Kingdom of the Mops.

Chapter 7. The Kingdom of the Mops.

The Kingdom of the Mops. A massive open cave with lanterns hanging from the walls. There were shelves cut into the rocks on which there were hundreds – thousands? – of mops. And in the middle of it all lay a throne, encrusted with jewels. And on the throne sat Arnold.

"There's Arnold!" cried Rudolph.

"What is he doing on there?" asked Sidney.

"It looks like he's their king!" suggested Ralph.

The mops were extremely surprised by the appearance of the submarine. They started swimming around very quickly in different directions, banging into one another as they did.

"I think we've startled them," Jeffrey said.

"They don't realise it's us!" added Derek.

Mr Parsnip turned on the ship's announcement system and his big voice boomed out into the cave. "Hello mops! No need to worry. This is Mr Parsnip and Class 9. We have come to find Arnold!"

This message calmed the mops down and instead of trying to swim away from the submarine they swum up to it to look in through the windows.

"Look, there's Blub!" said Keith.

"And there's Blub!" added Mark. Those two had given the mops names. They'd called them all 'Blub' because they couldn't tell the difference between them.

This had really annoyed Arnold who'd told them off, "They are all very different. You just have to look at them. This one is called Schminky and this one is called Pinky and this one ..."

"Yes, all right, Arnold, thanks," they said and they continued to call all of them 'Blub'.

The little moppy creatures pushed up against the windows of the submarine. The kids could see their black and white eyes poking out, almost popping out of their sockets. After having spent a week with them, they could tell this meant they were excited and glad. The Mops were excited and glad that they had gotten to see Class 9 again.

Mr Parsnip came into the main part of the submarine.

"What now?" Sidney asked.

"We go out there," Parsnip replied.

"How?"

"Put on the diving suits!"

At the back of the submarine were two large wardrobes which if you opened them, turned out to have diving suits in.

Mrs Pear and Miss Beetroot gave them out, then the children put them on. They spent a few moments parading up and down in delight in front of each other, but they didn't have too long for that cos there was serious business to be accomplished.

They went into the entry hatch five at a time. The inner door, to the submarine was then closed while the outer one was opened and the children swam out. The hatch was then closed, the water drained and the whole process repeated several times until nearly everyone was outside. Miss Beetroot stayed with the submarine to look after it.

Then they all swam over to Arnold's throne. He was sitting there quite coolly. It didn't seem as if he was bothered about all of the trouble he had caused.

"Arnold!" said Mr Parsnip. "What on earth do you think you're doing!? You cannot live under the sea with the mops! What would your mum think about it all!?"

Mention of Arnold's mum slightly wiped the smug look off his face but he still replied, "I have decided I am going to live here with them. They are my special friends. Only I can talk to them. Only I can understand them!"

"Right …" thought Mr Parsnip. Arnold had always been a stubborn lad. It was impossible to get him to do anything he didn't want to. This could be tricky. "Jeffrey, you go and talk to him," he suggested to one of Arnold's closest friends.

"Come on, Arnold!" said Jeff. "You can't stay here under the waves. We would miss you too much."

"Yes, come on, Arnold," added Dizzy.

Arnold looked round at all of his classmates who he loved dearly. He saw how much trouble they had gone to to come and rescue him. And Mr Parsnip, Mrs Pear and Miss Beetroot also.

But then he looked at the mops. They were strange creatures who had lived underwater for hundreds of years. It was the first time they had ever ventured onto the land. And he was the only one who could understand them.

It was a difficult choice. He gazed at the children. And then he gazed at the mops.

Then he said, "I'm gonna stay here."

Chapter 8. Schminky.

This was a problem. Mr Parsnip could not allow Arnold to stay there. He would lose his job; Arnold's parents would call the police; it would be very very bad in lots of ways. He must have been very stressed but he didn't show it. Instead, he looked as calm as ice while inside his brain was whirring at a hundred miles an hour.

"That's fair enough then, Arnold," he said. "Good luck with all that."

"Thanks," replied Arnold, a bit puzzled that Mr Parsnip had given up so easily.

"I just need you to do one thing before we go."

"What's that?"

"Write a letter to your Mum explaining why you're staying here."

"Oh," said Arnold.

"Yes, I mean, that's the least you could do if you're never going to see her again, isn't it?

"I suppose so."

"I've got some paper and a pen for you," said Mr P.

"Right ..." said Arnold.

"Go on then," said Mr P.

Arnold didn't like writing at the best of times. He'd already had to write one note that day to explain to his class where he'd gone. And now he was going to have to write another one. To his Mum. Who would miss him.

"Dear Mum," he wrote. "Dear Mum …" How could he put it? How could he explain so that she would understand? She would understand, wouldn't she that it was his job to look after the mops, that they needed him. That it was far more important for him to do that than to go to stupid old school. Maybe she could come and visit him? Though he knew that his Mum would never come and visit him all the way under the sea.

"Come on, Arnold, finish your letter. We need to be going," said Mr Parsnip. All Arnold had written so far was, "Dear Mum."

"I don't know if I can," he said.

"There is another possibility," added the teacher.

"What?" thought everyone in the class with sudden hope.

"Do you remember the portal?" Mr Parsnip asked.

"Yes," said Arnold. Of course he remembered it – the portal in Pinkerton School's staff room that had led to the Rinky Dinky's spaceship.

"I can make the portal point to anywhere. Instead of the Rinky-Dinkies' spaceship, which has gone now anyway, I could point it to here. Then you could come back with us and live with your Mum but you could visit here any time you wanted. How about that?"

"Wow!" cried Arnold.

"Wow!" went everyone. That was a great idea! Mr Parsnip had really come up with the goods!

"So you would let me come and visit the mops whenever I wanted to?" asked Arnold.

"Well, I don't know about whenever you wanted, but you could certainly come and visit," said Mr P.

"Hmmm …" thought Arnold. "Hmmm …" He was obstinate but he recognised a good thing when he saw one. So he said, "All right then!"

All right!! "Phew!" went everyone. Thank goodness for that! It would've been really bad if they'd had to've left Arnold there. But Mr Parsnip had found a way to get him to come back.

Arnold went round and said goodbye to the mops. All it sounded like he was saying was, "Blub blub," but the mops understood it and they replied "Blub blub," too.

The creatures wrapped their strings around him and he hugged them back.

The other children waited and watched until he was done. There was no hurry – after all, it would probably be a while before they were at the bottom of the ocean witnessing a scene like this. And they were all fond of the mops as well. It was nice to see them for one last time.

He came to the last mop, hugged it, said, "Blub blub". The mop said, "Blub blub" back, then Arnold said "Blub blub blub!".

Then the mop said, "Blub blub blub blub!" The two of them carried on talking like this for ages. Then Arnold and the mop swam over to Mr P.

"There's one more thing," he said.

"What's that?"

"This mop is coming with me."

"WHAT!!??" screeched Mr P.

"Schminky is coming with me," said Arnold.

"Schminky is not coming with you. He's a monster. We can't have monsters hanging around the school or going to your home!"

"He could be disguised as a mop," said Arnold.

Hmmm ... well, that wasn't a bad idea. Schminky and Pinky and Flinky all looked like mops, apart from the little black eyes, and when they closed those, they looked 100% like mops.

"He can live in the school cleaning cupboard with the other mops," said Arnold and he had that determined look on his face.

Mr Parsnip was not happy but he didn't have the time to argue with Arnold. "Fine!" he snarled, angrily.

Arnold didn't care that Mr Parsnip was upset – he was just overjoyed that he'd be able to take his new friend home with him.

"Blub blub blub," he said to the creature, which in mop language means, "Come on, Schminky!"

There was then another lengthy scene where Schminky went round saying goodbye to all the other mops.

"Can we get a move on, please, Arnold!?" screamed Mr P. He was so cross he was about to explode.

"Come on, Schminky!" Arnold said again. "We have to go." The Plinky-Plonky finished hugging the last of his mates then swam over and joined Class 9.

“Let’s go then!” said Mr P. He set off for the submarine, the children and Schminky followed him, and Mrs Pear came last.

“Hello, everyone!” trilled Miss Beetroot joyfully as she welcomed them back into the craft. “Oh, and who’s this?” she asked, surprised as the mop came through.

“It’s Schminky,” said Arnold.

“Oh, hello, Schminky!” said Miss B.

Everybody – apart from Schminky - took off their diving suits and resumed their seats. Miss Beetroot handed out orange squash and biscuits to everyone. She wasn’t sure what Schminky wanted.

“He’ll just have some water please,” said Arnold.

“Oh, all right then,” Miss Beetroot replied and she went to fetch the mop some water.

Arnold sat next to Schminky. Mr Parsnip went up the front to the cockpit and began to drive them back to Colwyn Bay. First of all, he had to turn the machine around. Then they headed back down the dark tunnel they’d travelled through, into the sea. Then up and up through the water until they landed on the beach.

The AA had been to fix the coach's wheel so, after a quick toilet stop, the children piled straight on to the bus.

"Can't we just go through the portal?" Sidney asked Mr Parsnip.

"I'm afraid not," the teacher replied. "Mr Loaf and all of the parents will be expecting a coach to come back, so that's what we have to do. The portal has to remain a secret. Anyway, I can't reprogram it from this end, I need to do that from Pinkerton."

"Oh well, fair enough," thought Sidney although he was highly excited about the prospect of using the portal again. "Can we use it to go places as well as Arnold, please?" he asked.

"Oh, man!" sighed Mr Parsnip. "See, this is why I kept it a secret. Now everyone's going to want a go."

"Yes, please!" said Su. "Can we go to Disneyland?"

"Yes, please!" cried Bob. "Can we go to Brazil and play football on the beach?"

"Yes, please!" said Vanessa. "I'd like to go to Dog World and meet all the dogs!"

"There is no such place as 'Dog World'!" said Mr Parsnip, "and the answer to all of you is 'no'. The portal has a limited amount of energy. It's not for us to have fun with. It's for more important things than that!"

"Ohhhhh!" went Su, Bob and Vanessa. Later on the coach, they said to each other, "It's not fair that Arnold gets to use the portal just because he throws a massive strop and heads off under the sea. That doesn't seem fair at all! What about us?"

What indeed? Those three children spent the entire journey back to Pinkerton musing on the injustice of it all as well as coming up with ever new destinations they'd like the portal to take them to. By the time the coach rolled up in front of the school gates, Su, Bob and Vanessa were determined they would have to get their hands on that portal one way or another.

Chapter 9. Back home.

The journey back took about five hours. Arnold gazed out of the window some of the time; chatted with Schminky some of the time. He was going home. Back to see his Mum. He was leaving behind the mops and Colwyn Bay. But he had a new friend – Schminky. How was that going to work out? he wondered.

The only thing the others were talking about was Arnold and Schminky.

"How did he breathe down there?" Dizzy asked Trin.

"I don't know," replied the drizzle-haired kid.

"Why hasn't Mr Parsnip told him off!?" asked Keith. "If we did that, we'd be in a whole load of grief!!"

"I'm sure he will tell him off," said Mark. "We just need to get him home first."

"We're actually gonna have a live monster at school!" said Nancy. "That is so-o cool!"

"I know, right?" agreed Nedrun. "I hope Arnold will let us play with it."

"Yeah," said Tina, "I hope he doesn't just keep it to himself!"

Conversations like that filled the journey and before they knew it, they were back in Pinkerton.

All the parents were waiting for them as the coach pulled in to the car park. "Yayyyy!" they cried and waved. Their faces were so glad to see their babies again after having been without them for five days.

The kids were glad to see their parents too, noses pushed up against the coach windows and before long they were tumbling down the stairs and into their Mum's and Dad's arms.

Mr Parsnip, Mrs Pear and Miss Beetroot looked on. They checked that everyone's parents were there, waited for them all to leave, then Mrs Pear said, "I'd better be off. Mr Pear will be waiting for me."

"Thanks very much for everything you've done this week," said Mr P and then the older TA made her way along the path in the descending gloom towards her car, leaving just Mr Parsnip and Miss Beetroot behind. And the Mop. Arnold had gone home with his mum and left the mop behind!

"Oh well, Schminky," said Mr Parsnip, "looks like you're coming home with me!"

"Are you going to be all right with that thing!?" Miss Beetroot asked.

"Don't call it a thing!" he rebuked her.

"What shall I call it?"

"A beast!" he said.

"All the best with the beast then," she said and then she walked along the lane too to her little car leaving Mr Parsnip and Schminky behind.

The man and the monster alone in the car park of Pinkerton Primary School. It was a long way from home. Schminky looked a little bit freaked-out, bless him.

"It's all right, Schminky!" Mr Parsnip said gently. What he actually said was, "Blub blub blub." The teacher had learned a bit of their language – nowhere near as much as Arnold – but enough to say that.

"Blub blub blub!" replied Schminky tearfully. Mr Parsnip didn't understand that but he guessed it probably meant something like, "This is weird, isn't it? Have I made the right decision? I hope so, but I'm not sure. And where is King Arnold!!??" The mop looked up at him with big round eyes.

"Come on, Schmink!" Parsnip said again. The man ruffled the monster's fronds, then headed towards his car, the only one left. Schminky, Plinky-Plonky slithered behind.

Chapter 10. Pirates.

That spring was amazing. You've no idea how much having a monster around livens things up. Maths lessons suddenly became much more interesting. English lessons were brilliant anyway but with a monster around, they became the best thing ever!!

Schminky was very cute and affectionate. He would run around the room giving hugs to everyone, then he'd stop in the middle of the room and do a little dance. Mr Parsnip would put on some music – Lady Gaga seemed to be his favourite – and the little beastie would shake his mop.

When it came to home time, Schminky would stay behind with Mr P. Parsnip would do his marking, tidy up, and by that time all the other teachers had gone. He and Schmink would make their way out to the car. They'd go back to Parsnip's place and Schminky would get in the bathtub.

After a few days, the teacher said to Arnold, "I thought you were supposed to be looking after him!"

"My Mum won't let me."

"Have you asked?"

"I can't ask her if I can have a monster in the house! She'd think I was insane!"

"So I have to look after him!?"

"You're used to monsters, Mr Parsnip from what you tell us. Like the Dooby-Doos – you know, with the two heads and the really blue skin. The long wavy arms. You told us all about how you fought them in the intergalactic wars. And won! Surely a little mop can't be any trouble?"

The boy had a point. Mr Parsnip lived on his own and sometimes was lonely. It was nice to have company. Though he still couldn't work out how to speak mop.

"How did you learn to speak their language?" he asked Arnold.

"I didn't learn," said Steenburgen. "I just knew it anyway."

"And how did you manage to breathe underwater?"

"Dunno," the lad answered.

Arnold was not normally keen on English lessons but one day he offered to make a presentation to the whole class.

"What about?" asked Mr P.

"Mops," replied A.

Well, that should be interesting, thought Parsnip. I wonder what Schminky has been telling him?

So they gave the lesson over to Arnold and he explained to them the story of the Mops.

"Two hundred years ago, there was a pirate ship called the Black Widow."

"Ooh," whispered Kay to Susie, "I love stories about pirates!"

"The captain was a man called Long John Hopscotch. He was a fearsome pirate who ruled the seven seas. He travelled wherever he wanted and stole whatever he liked. No-one dared defy him."

"But one night, the Black Widow ran into a terrible storm, the worst storm he and his men had ever seen. It tore the ship apart. All the pirates plunged to their deaths."

"This is a good story," said Keith, "but what's it got to do with the Mops?"

"On the ship was a whole load of Mops in a wooden crate. In the next crate was a mysterious magical potion Long John had picked up in the islands of Vanuatu.

When the storm broke the boat in half, the wooden crates smashed …"

"And the Mops and the potion got mixed up?" guessed Dizzy.

"Exactly!" said Arnold. "The Mops and the potion got mixed up. Then they were hit by lightning and the Mops came to life! They've lived under the ocean ever since!"

Wow, that was quite a story, thought everyone, and it gave them loads to think about and write about for the next few lessons.

Mr Loaf, the headteacher looked at their work. "Your children have quite an imagination!" he complimented Mr Parsnip though he didn't realise it wasn't fiction he was reading, it was FACT!!

Arnold didn't normally do much writing. Ordinarily, he'd just scrawl a couple of lines. Since he'd met Schminky though, he'd started writing loads. The only problem was it was in Mop.

His latest piece was about Long John Hopscotch and it read:

Blub blub blub. Blub blub blub blub, blub, blub blub!!

Blub. Blub, blub, blub.

"Blub?"

"Blub blub blub!"

BLUB BLUB BLUB BLUB!

And so on. You get the idea. This went on for ten pages. Arnold now wrote by far the most in the class. Unfortunately it was just the word, "Blub"!

"What is this?" Mr Parsnip asked him.

"It's Mop."

"I can't read Mop."

"That's your problem!"

"No it's not! It's your problem cos I'm going to give this zero unless you write it in English!"

"Give it zero then. See if I care!"

Parsnip did give it zero. And Arnold didn't care.

Chapter 11. Par-tay!!

Class 9 had a party at Sidney Brown's house. All the children came, Mr Parsnip, Mrs Beetroot, Mrs Pear. And Schminky. Sidney's dad put on the barbeque and there were loads of hamburgers and sausages for everyone. The sun was hot and people jumped into the pool Sidney had in his garden.

Schminky loved it. Since he'd been in Pinkerton, the most water he'd had had been in Mr Parsnip's bathtub, which was all right – it was warm and soapy – but it was a bit small. There wasn't room for him to swim around and he loved swimming.

So when he saw Sidney's pool, he went insane. "Wheeeeee!!" the monster cried and threw himself into the pool straight on top of Tyke and Keith.

"Ug!" they went as they sucked up his straggly fronds but it wasn't for long, for Schminky was off, swimming really fast through the pool. He was mostly underwater – they could just see a little bit of the top of his head peeking through. The children got out of his way as he zoomed this way and that, that way and this for half an hour non-stop.

Eddie ate some hamburgers; Ralph munched on chicken wings. They talked about Wales. "Those were good times!" said Eddie.

"Sure were," agreed Ralph.

Schminky came back onto the land and dashed round to each member of Class 9. They patted him. He smiled and gurgled.

Then he told Arnold that he wanted to go back.

"What!?" asked Arnold.

"I want to go back."

The thing was, Schminky explained, Mops love water. They love swimming in it. They need loads of water so they can swim properly. Schminky had told himself that he'd be all right in Pinkerton. He loved the kids so much – especially Arnold – but when he'd got into the swimming pool, it was as if he'd gone home again, into the deeps. Back into the deep blue sea of Colwyn Bay.

"Blub," he said to Arnold, which meant, in Mop language, "Sorry!"

"It's ok," said Arnold.

They went to Mr Parsnip and told him what Schminky had said. Mr Parsnip agreed they could use the portal the next day.

Chapter 12. Back to Colwyn Bay.

They had get the staff out of the staff room so they could use the portal. That wasn't going to be easy. Someone was always in there, drinking coffee or eating biscuits!

Trinny hit on an idea though. "What about if we get a helicopter to land on the field next door and have some celebrity in it? Then everyone would go out to see who it was."

"Good idea!" reckoned Tim. "My Dad's got a helicopter!"

"And my Mum is best friends with Harry Kane!" said Dizzy.

So it was that the next day, Harry Kane, England football captain, flew in to Pinkerton Primary School in a helicopter. Mr Schnorbitz, the caretaker, saw him first. He rushed into the office and gave them the news. Mr Loaf declared, "Right, school cancelled! Harry Kane is here (for some reason). Let's go out and see him!" And every single person in the school rushed out to meet the superstar.

Everyone apart from Schminky, Parsnip and Arnold Steenburgen. They entered the staff room. There, behind the water machine was the portal, shimmering away. Of course, if you didn't know to look for it, you wouldn't see it. The teachers and the TAs sat in there everyday without noticing. But Mr Parsnip and Arnold saw it straightaway.

Last time they'd been through, it had led to the Rinky-Dinkies' spaceship. But Mr P had changed the frequency and now it pointed at Colwyn Bay. "Ready?" he asked. Arnold and the Mop nodded and they stepped through. Onto the beach at Colwyn Bay.

It was deserted. There was no-one around. "That's weird!" Mr Parsnip said. "The Mops were supposed to be meeting us here. I sent a message. I wonder where they are." They had a look round, along the beach, behind the sand dunes, into the playground but the Mops were nowhere to be found.

"Let's go back to the house where we stayed," suggested Arnold. "Maybe they've gone there."

So the three of them climbed a hill to the cottage. Mr Parsnip knocked on the door. It took a while – they thought maybe no-one was in – but then there was a noise, the latch turned and it opened to reveal Ronald Fish.

"Mr Fish, how are you?" said Mr P.

"Ah, Mr Parsnip, isn't it?" replied the strange man.

"Yes, that's right."

"What brings you back so soon?"

Parsnip thought back to the last time he'd seen Ronald Fish. It was the night the Mops had attacked. He'd watched Fish run, screaming out of the door of his house. Fish knew about the Mops. So Mr Parsnip could mention them.

"We're looking for the Mops."

"The Mops ..." went Fish, as if he was trying to remember.

"You know, the monsters who came out of the sea!"

"Oh, yes," replied Fish with a creepy little smile, which was weird cos they'd thought he was scared of them.

"Have you seen them?" Arnold asked, desperately. He wanted to see his old friends.

"No, no, no," replied Fish. "Well, there's one there!" he said, pointing at Schminky, and then he chuckled again.

This was all very odd. Why did the man keep on laughing!? There was nothing funny about the situation at all! Perhaps he was just weird – some people just are.

"Oh well, thanks very much," said P and off they went, back to the beach.

"What are we going to do now?" asked Arnold.

"Get the submarine!" suggested Parsnip. He dialled it up and it started to surge through the sea towards Colwyn Bay. The yellow machine appeared majestically from under the waves. Parsnip, Arnold and Schminky rushed towards it and got in.

The yellow submarine zoomed through the sea towards the Mops' underground lair. "They'll be there!" Arnold told himself over and over again. He pictured them from when he'd been there, swimming happily around in the cave, going "blub, blub". He'd sat in the middle, on the throne. They all kept coming up to him and looked at him with such love! And hugging him – sometimes there were twenty of them on top of him, one after the other would pile on top. It was such good fun!!

They'd be there, he knew it, and he couldn't wait to see them again.

The submarine got to the bottom of the ocean and slowed down. This was the tricky bit – it had to ease along carefully, make sure it didn't hit any of the bits of rock and then go gently up and through the tunnel, into the cave.

The crystals in the rock sparkled. The submarine safely made its way through to the cave.

And it was empty.

There were no Mops there. There was no-one there at all. Arnold rushed to the hatch, opened it and swam out. He didn't need a diving suit. He swam around the cave looking for his friends. But he couldn't find them.

He spent a long time looking even after he'd searched each part of the cave five times. He just kept on looking. But they weren't there. In the end, he returned to the submarine. "They're gone," he said to Mr Parsnip and to Schminky. "They're gone. The Mops have disappeared."

Chapter 13. Fish.

"It's all right, Arnold, I know what to do," said Mr Parsnip even though he had no idea what to do at all!! He felt he had to say something encouraging though, the boy was so sad.

"What do we do?" asked Arnold.

"Well, … let's go back to shore first. I'll tell you then!" replied Parsnip just to give himself time to think. He took off the submarine's brake, put it into gear, then started turning the wheel around, moved the submarine around, then got it out of there, through the bright blue ocean past a million and one fish swimming gaily, enjoying their lives, back towards Colwyn Bay and all the while he was trying to work out, "Where are the Mops?"

Where were they? It didn't make sense. They'd lived under the ocean for two hundred years. Why would they suddenly disappear? His mind was a blank. The submarine was zooming towards the coast and he hadn't got a single thing to say to Arnold.

It was just as well then that the boy himself had thought of something. "I've got an idea," he told Mr P.

"What is it?"

"Follow fish," said the boy.

“Fish!? Which fish? There are loads of them! The pink one? The red one? The yellow and orange one??”

“No!” said Arnold. “*Ronald* Fish.”

Ah! *Ronald* Fish, the man! “Why?” he asked.

“Because he knows something.”

“Yes,” thought the teacher. Obviously, he obviously knows something, the strange way he was behaving earlier. So, follow him. See where he goes. Now, that was a good idea. Why couldn’t he have thought of that!? Hmmm, he must be getting slow in his old age. Anyway, it didn’t matter cos Arnold had thought of it and hopefully it might lead them to the Mops.

The two humans and the Mop hid behind the sand dune near to the house. The lights were on, they could see Ronald Fish inside moving from one room to another. After a while, they saw him go into the hall and put his coat on. He was leaving!

And indeed he was. Ronald opened the door to the house, stepped outside, walked over to his car and drove away.

Parsnip, Arnold and Schminky meanwhile hopped on a magical skateboard the teacher had popped back through the portal for, and followed at a safe distance.

The little green car that Fish was driving wove its way through the tiny town of Colwyn Bay, in and out, up and down the roads of the seaside resort, then it left it altogether and got onto the A547. The skateboard followed behind.

"Where's he going?" wondered Mr P.

The green car picked up speed and so did the skateboard. Before long they were dashing along at 70 mph! That was pretty windy for a skateboard!! Parsnip felt sick but Arnold was driving and he was ok.

Schminky sat on top of Arnold's head and the strands of the Mop were swept backwards by the air-flow. This was great fun, it thought, almost as good as being underwater! Mr P did not think it was good fun. It was all he could do to avoid falling off.

Fish was now driving very fast, at about 100 miles per hour, in and out of the traffic. The skateboard could not keep up. It nearly collided with a lorry – had to go underneath it! – they were gonna lose him – then they saw him signal to turn off the A547, slow down and head to a shopping centre. The gang was able to catch up and arrived just in time to see him heading for the shops.

"He's going shopping!" said Parsnip. "We've wasted all this time following him and he's simply going to buy stuff!"

"No, there's something fishy about it," said Arnold. He got off the skateboard, parked it, then walked towards the shops. Parsnip and Schminky came too.

There was a massive sign above the door that read, "North Wales Shopping Centre". The place was enormous and brilliant with light. But it was closed. The humans looked at their watches. Five past nine. A sign on the door said that it closed at nine. Why had Ronald Fish come here then? And where was he? Had he made it inside before they shut the doors? They peered inside to see if they could spot him but they couldn't.

Then they looked around outside and, far away, down to the right of the shopping centre, they saw a shadow walking along. It must be him! And then it was gone! Like magic!

They hurried along by the side of the shopping centre to where they'd seen him. There were no lights. It was pretty gloomy. Perhaps he was lurking in the shadows, ready to jump out at them. They proceeded with care. But he wasn't there. Where had he gone to!?

Schminky saw it - a door in the corner, ajar. “Blub blub!” the creature told Arnold.

“He must’ve gone through there!” said the boy. Mysterious! What was Fish up to? There was only one way to find out.

Chapter 14. MOPS!!

The gang opened up the door and went through. Beyond, it was pitch black. "Walk slowly!" ordered Arnold. "And follow me!"

They did as the boy suggested and very bravely stepped into the dark. Who knew what manner of things might be there? Monsters of every kind! Vampires, demons and werewolves quite possibly. Rinky-Dinkies maybe. It was very frightening. But they carried on nonetheless.

At one point, Arnold trod on a thing that made a huge CRACK!! The three of them leapt about hundred feet in the air! They were going to scream and it was only amazing levels of self-control that stopped them. They didn't want to alert anyone – or any*thing* - else that they were there.

Soon after that though, it started getting lighter. They could see where they were going. They could look around and they could see that they were just in a normal corridor and that there were no monsters of any kind. Up ahead was another door, slightly open and from behind that one spilt light. It was that slither of light which illuminated them now.

Arnold marched forward. He'd had enough of this nonsense now, didn't hesitate, opened the door wide. Into the shopping centre.

There were a few shoppers left, most of them were making their way to the exits. A voice came over the loudspeakers – "Please would all shoppers leave. The shopping centre is closed." 'Next', 'Marks and Spencer' and 'Clintons Cards' began to roll their shutters down.

Where was Ronald Fish and what was he up to? The three of them decided to hide behind a pillar and see what happened. The last couple of shoppers trickled off, then the whole place became empty.

Then Ronald Fish came out. He stood in the middle of the floor with a ridiculous sneer on his face, gazed around proudly and gave an enormous cry – "MOPS!!!"

Then from every corner the Mops appeared, scuttling across the floor towards Ronald Fish. So that was where they were!! He then cried out again another single word – "CLEAN!!!" – and the Mops dispersed. Some of them went out of sight; a few remained in view and they started to clean the floor. Fish patrolled around with a mean look on his face, occasionally shouting things like, "Work harder!" and "Get on with it or else!" and then the Mops would clean even more quickly.

They were fast anyway and unlike normal mops they didn't need humans to work them. They zoomed around and after about fifteen minutes, were done. They came back into the middle of the floor around Fish and he gave them another order, "Back to your cages!" and off they went, leaving him alone. He walked around the floor a bit for a while, inspecting it to check it was clean, then he headed back to the door he, Parsnip, Arnold and Schminky had come through. He exited through it, closed it behind himself and then he was gone.

"So, that's where they are!" said Mr P.

"I told you there was something suspicious about him!" replied Arnold.

"Blub blub!" said Schminky.

"Come on then!" said Arnold.

"Where are we going?"

"To get them out of their cages!"

Schminky was able to follow the scent of the beasts through the shopping centre. They went past Sainsburys and "Build-a-Bear"; past "Sports Direct" and "Game" until they came to a gate. A massive iron gate which was locked. The three of them peered through – it was dark beyond – they couldn't see much but if they strained their ears they could hear the mournful sound, "Blub blub."

"Blub blub. Blub blub. Blub blub."

Their friends were in there!! Behind the iron gate - but how could they get through? Arnold and Parsnip examined the gate, they shook it, but it was shut fast. They had no way of opening it.

"What are we going to do?" Arnold asked.

"I don't know," Mr Parsnip admitted.

"Blub blub," said Schminky.

Chapter 15. Reinforcements.

What they did do was get back on the skateboard and head to Colwyn Bay. They zoomed along the A547, in and out of the traffic, then into the town itself. It was night-time now – there were very few people around. They easily made their way back to the beach.

"Time to call in reinforcements," said Mr P.

The three of them went through the portal, back into the staff room. Parsnip and Schmink dropped Arnold off at his Mum's, then went back to the teacher's place. The monster got into the bath and Mr P sat in his lounge and planned. He drank a pint of beer and ate a curry and tried to come up with a scheme to rescue the Mops.

The next day, Class 9 was reunited in their classroom. They cancelled lessons for the day – there was something much more important to be discussed.

"How was Harry Kane?" Arnold asked.

"Amazing, thanks!" Dizzy replied.

"Yes," Bob said, "we had a football match – all of us against him."

"Who won?"

"He did. Ten-nil!"

"Oh no!!!"

"Yeah. It was all right though. I mean, he is one of the best players in the world!"

"Yeah!"

"And how was your trip?"

"Well …" said Arnold and then he laid it out. Everything. Ronald Fish, the shopping centre, the cages …

"Oh no!" said Charmaine. "What are we going to do?"

"Well," replied Mr P. "It's like this … We'll need to wait until they come out of their cages tonight. Then I'll go and distract Fish and you guys can get the Mops."

"Are we all going?" asked Charmaine.

"Yes!" said the man.

"Brilliant!" cried the girl.

"Brilliant!" shouted Tyke.

"Fantastic!" hollered Trin.

There were a couple of problems to overcome before they'd be able to do this though. Mainly, how could 30 nine year olds get to stay out that late??

Ricky had the answer. "My Mum knows the Rolling Stones. I'll get her to ask them to stage a concert here tonight on the Pinkerton playing fields. Everyone will come. While they're doing that, we can go into the portal."

"Good idea!" agreed Sidney Brown. He knew his parents were crazy about the Stones and they'd want to come.

"Who are the Rolling Stones?" asked Susie.

"They're a rock band. Very famous. All the Mums and Dads like 'em."

"Ok then," she said. It sounded like a plan.

Ricky's Mum rung up Mick Jagger (the lead singer of the Stones)

"Hi, Mick!"

"Is that Cynthia?"

"Yes."

"Long time no see. How ya doin' baby?"

"Listen, Mick, I need you to do me a favour …"

"What's that?"

"Play a concert tonight at Pinkerton."

"Ok, baby, sure, yep, I can do that."

“Thanks, Mick!”

“No problems, man.”

So it was arranged. The Rolling Stones came to Pinkerton. The whole village crowded onto the playing field to watch. And Class 9 sneaked into the staff room while it was going on.

“We’ve got to hurry!” said Mr P. He’d adjusted the portal so it pointed to just outside the shopping centre. They all slipped through, one after the other, into the corner of the staff room, behind the water machine, and then out, to North Wales. When they’d all come through, Mr P pointed them to the door on the side of the building. It was open. They entered. The time was five past nine – the same time as they’d visited the night before. All the shops were closing up. Again, there were a few people left doing their last bits of shopping. But they too would soon be gone. And then it would be the Time of the Mops.

It happened as it had the night before. The voice came over the loudspeaker – “The shops are closing now; please leave the shopping centre!” The last few people disappeared and then Ronald Fish emerged. He strode into the middle of the centre and cried out, “MOPS!!” and the Mops came from their cages – dozens of them. They gathered around the strange fellow.

It was at this point that Mr Parsnip stepped out.

"Mr Fish!" he cried. "How nice to see you! What are you doing here?" The teacher strode right over to the strange man and grabbed hold of his hand to shake it.

You should have seen the look on Fish's face!! He wasn't smirking any more, that was for sure! He was totally astonished.

Parsnip took advantage of Fish's surprise. He took a hold of the man and drew him to one side. "I'm glad I've met you here," he said, "there's something I really need to talk to you about. Let's go for a little walk, shall we?" Mr Parsnip could be very forceful when he wanted to and Fish had little choice other than to obey. The two guys went for a walk in the direction of the big sweet shop and before long were out of sight.

"This is it!" cried Arnold. "Everyone grab a Mop!"

The children of Class 9 ran towards the Mops. It seemed they would need to take 2 or 3 each but that shouldn't be a problem.

Mark went up to one of them and whispered, "Hi, Mop, it's me, Mark. Do you remember? We've come to rescue you. You just need to come with us."

Tina ran up to another and said, "Hi, Moppy! How are you? It's me, Tina. Quick come with me and I'll help you escape!"

Arnold ran up to the Mop he knew was called Ludwig van Beethoven and said, "Blub blub!" which meant pretty much the same thing as Mark and Tina had said.

Ludwig looked back at him and said, "Blub blub." Which meant, "Who are you?"

Chapter 16. Red eyes.

Arnold said, “Blub blub,” which means in Mop language, “What do you mean, ‘who am I?’? I’m Arnold Steenburgen. I was your King!! Don’t you remember??”

Ludwig looked back at him with cold, dead eyes and said, “Blub.” Which means, “No.”

WHAT WAS GOING ON!!!???

How could they not remember King Arnold of the Mops!!??

The other children couldn’t understand what the Mops were saying to them but they did realise that the beasts didn’t want to come with them. Why not??? It was puzzling. Eddie grabbed hold of a string of one of the Mops. He was gonna pull it out of there if he had to! But that turned out not to be a good idea!

The Mop’s eyes went red. It squealed “BLUB BLUB!!” at the top of its voice and leapt on top of Eddie. All the other Mops did the same to the children they were near. And this time they were not hugging them, they were attacking!!

Fortunately for the children, Mops don’t have claws. Nor sharp teeth. So they can’t attack with those. The way they do attack is jump up in the air and then squelch down on their prey. And they do that over and over again, all the while screaming, "BLUB BLUB BLUB BLUB BLUB BLUB BLUB BLUB BLUB BLUB BLUBBBBBBBBBBBBBB!!!" There were two or three Mops per child so it was quite an assault. What made it worse was that it was a surprise – no-one had been expecting it.

After a few minutes of this, all the children were lying on the floor, some of them curled up into balls, others crying, all of them defeated. The Mops sensed this and their mad attack came to an end. They climbed off the bodies of the prone children and stood to the side in case the kids tried anything. But the kids weren't going to try anything. They were half-dead.

And Ronald Fish walked back in. "Ah, Class 9! Nice to see you!! How are you all?" he sighed. He was talking to himself really – none of the kids could manage to speak, so Fish continued.

"I presume you came here to rescue the Mops from my evil grasp, did you?" (Again, no response from the devastated kids) "We-e-e-lll …" he went and then he did an evil laugh (which, to be fair, was a pretty good one. It sounded natural – as if he was genuinely having a good time – which is the key), "… what if they don't want to be rescued???" Then he did another enormous, really evil schmeevil weevil laugh that chilled the children's souls down to the bone. "Wa-ha-ha-ha-ha-ha-ha-ha-haaaaaaaaaaaa!!!!" it went.

"Oooooo-hoooooooooooo-hoooooooooo!!" he carried on. "Eeeeeeeeeeeeeeeeeeeeeeeeeeeee!! Hubba-lubba-bubba-wubba-schmubba-dubba. Hoolie, boolie, wap, wap wap wap …" and so on and so on, on and on and on until Ricky summoned up the energy to cry out, "WILL YOU PLEASE SHUT UP!!??" after which he collapsed again on the floor.

There was silence. At least Ricky had managed to stop Fish laughing. Instead, he spoke. "The Mops want to be with me. They like being with me!!! Don't you, Mops?" he asked them.

"Blub blub," they replied which means, "Yes, we do, Master!"

"Why?" asked Su.

"They found you annoying. Silly little children, they said. I agree. You are silly little children. Now run along before you get hurt any more."

"Where's Mr Parsnip?" asked Keith.

"Oh, don't you worry about him," sneered Fish. "He's all right. Run along now, there's good little kids!" The Mops pushed against the children, who were still lying on the floor, rolling them over and over, towards the door.

The kids were upset and confused. "GET OUT!!!" screamed Ronald. It didn't seem like they had any choice. So they left. They slunk back through the door, into the corridor, then out of the other door into the car park. Fish slammed the door shut.

Chapter 17. The watch.

Ronald Fish went back into the shopping centre where the Mops were waiting for him. "Well, what are you hanging about for!? CLEAN!!!" he screeched. And as he did, he held up a golden watch. It glinted in the lights. The Mops stared at it for a moment then began to clean, super-fast, even faster than before. They were desperate to clean, to please Ronald, to please the one who held the golden watch.

Last Spring, Ronald had been walking along the beach, not doing anything really, getting a breath of fresh air before another school party arrived. He'd seen something gleaming in the sand and leant over to pick up the golden watch. It was beautiful. There was a name inscribed on the back. Its owner, he guessed. "Long John Hopscotch," it read.

"Never heard of him," Fish thought, as he put the watch in his pocket, and that was where it stayed until the night the Mops attacked his house.

He ran outside, terrified for his life, fell over and found a Mop looming over him. "Waaaaaahhhh!" the man wailed. Frantically, he reached in his pocket for something, a weapon perhaps with which to fight the beast. And he took out the watch.

The second the Mop saw the watch it stopped dead still. Ronald was able to get up and move around and the Mop still stayed motionless. He poked it and still it didn't move.

"What is this!?" thought Ron. "Look at me!" he said to the Mop and it turned around and looked at him. "Fall over!" he ordered. The Mop fell down. "Jump in the air!" he cried and the Mop tried to do that.

"Well, well, well," he thought. "What have we got here? A slave!!!! I've got myself a slave! No!" he thought, "I've got myself a hundred slaves!" looking back in at the house. "Wa ha ha!" he went. It was his first evil laugh. It was pretty short and not terribly loud but it felt good. Ronald Fish was on his way to the dark side.

Fish waited for Class 9's holiday to end and then he stepped in. "Mops!" he cried as found them hanging around on the beach one day. He held up the golden watch and at once they snapped to attention. "Clean my house!" he said. It just came into his mind – after all, his house was very dirty – and they were mops, what else are mops for??

As soon as he gave the instruction, the hundred or so Mops swept towards the house and cleaned it. They were so fast they finished inside five minutes. Then they came back outside to their Master for more instructions.

The shopping centre idea came later on. "Where needs a lot of cleaning?" he wondered to himself. Then he saw an advert for cleaners at the North Wales Shopping Centre. He told them he could do the whole place super-cheap cos he knew he wouldn't have to pay the Mops anything. So they hired him. And the Mops cleaned it every night. And he took all the money.

A few months later, Class 9 had come back. But he'd sorted them out, no problem!

"What have we done????" cried Tyke. "We've left the Mops and Mr P in there with that bad man!!"

"We had no choice. The Mops were attacking us!" said Ricky.

"He was controlling them somehow!" reckoned Derek.

"Yes, the Mops are nice. They're our friends. Why would they suddenly turn on us?"

Mr Parsnip was in one of the Mops' cages. How could he have been so stupid? He was talking away to Fish, really pleased with himself that he'd managed to take him away from where the Mops were. Surely, the children would have rescued them by now, he thought. Then he saw a glint of something. Something gold. Fish took the watch from out of his pocket.

"It's pretty, isn't it?" he said.

"Yes," replied Mr P.

"Yesssssss," said Ronald soothingly and he led Mr Parsnip slowly and surely towards the cages. "Why don't you get in here?" he whispered to the teacher.

"Yes, all right, then," replied Parsnip. It seemed like the most reasonable thing in the world. He stepped into the cage and then Fish closed the door behind him. "Wa ha ha ha ha ha ha ha ha!" he laughed.

The children rattled the door of the shopping centre. It was locked. "We could break a window?" suggested Charmaine.

"Good idea!" cried Kay. She picked up a stone and threw it at one of the windows. Everyone gasped. That was reckless! Unfortunately, the stone bounced back off. It must be reinforced glass!

Parsnip rattled the door of his cage. It was locked tight. He tried calling out, "Help me, please!!! HELP!!!" but no-one could hear. Hmmmm, this was very bad indeed!

The children couldn't get in. Mr Parsnip couldn't get out. The Rolling Stones were about to finish their set – the parents would be getting ready to go home – looking around and wondering where their kids had got to.

All would have been lost if it hadn't been for … Schminky.

Schminky was inside the shopping centre. Fish didn't realise cos all the Mops looked the same to him. He also didn't realise that the golden watch didn't work on Schminky!

It would've done, a couple of months ago, but since then Schminky had been living with humans. It was almost as if he was part-human now. He saw the watch and thought, "That's nice!" but didn't feel he had to obey the one who was holding it.

No. He watched very carefully everything that happened. Fish putting Parsnip in a cage. His friends, the Mops, attacking his other friends, Class 9. And Ronald Fish presiding over it all with the watch. And he made a plan.

Chapter 18. Slither.

"COME ON MOPS!!! WORK HARDER!!!" screamed Fish as he walked around, inspecting their work. "YOU'VE MISSED A BIT!!!" he yelled at one of them who hurried back to the dirty mark.

Then he came to another Mop who was behaving strangely – it was just lying on the ground as if it were dead or at least very ill.

"GET UP!" cried Fish but the Mop did not obey.

"Hmmmm," thought Ronald. "He must be sick," and he bent over to examine the Mop. Then suddenly the creature leapt up and slithered all over him. Urghhhhh!! Ronald hated actually being touched by the beasts – they were so slimy! He drew back straightaway and got out a handkerchief to clean himself. Yuk!!! What was wrong with that Mop?

He needed the watch. If he showed it to the monster, it would shape up, get off the floor and do some cleaning, which was what mops were meant to do!

Now where had he put the watch? It was usually in his waistcoat pocket but it wasn't there. He must have put it in his trouser pocket instead. But, no, it wasn't in there. How about the other trouser pocket? No. Panic began to build within his chest. "Calm down," he told himself, "it must be somewhere. You only just had it a minute ago. Nothing has happened since then except …"

Except he was attacked by the beast. Where was the pesky varmint? He turned around to look for it but it had disappeared. Where had it gone!? He couldn't see it anywhere!!

And where was his watch? It wasn't in any of his pockets and it wasn't lying around on the ground.

It led him to the unavoidable conclusion: THE MOP HAD STOLEN THE WATCH!!!

"THE MOP HAS STOLEN THE WATCH!!" he cried out loud. "MOPS, GET HERE!!" he shouted but they didn't obey. They heard his voice but they didn't obey it. Because he didn't have the watch.

Because Schminky had it. His plan had worked perfectly. Pretend to be ill, get the man to lean over you, then steal the watch. Part 1 of the plan had gone like a dream.

Part 2 was to go and rescue Mr P.. Schminky hurried towards the cages. He went past his mop friends but didn’t have time to talk to them yet. That would be Part 3. No, Mr Parsnip came first.

There was a button that locked and opened all the cages all at once. Schminky jumped up and pressed it. The teacher sprang forth. “Thanks, Schmink,” he said. “What do we do now?”

“Blub blub,” the monster replied. Parsnip had no idea what it meant but it didn’t really matter cos the beast was already haring back to the shops. All P had to do was follow.

They met Fish by the entrance to WH Smith’s.

“GIVE ME BACK THAT WATCH!!” he yelled at Schminky.

“Blub,” replied the Mop. Parsnip understood that one. It meant, “No!”

“GIVE IT TO ME!!” Fish cried again and he ran at the beast to try and grab it off him.

“Blub,” the monster said. It sidestepped very smoothly just as Ronald lunged at it. (Mops are great at sliding around!)

Ronald gathered himself for another attack but then Schminky said, “BLUB!” At this, all the Mops in the shopping centre dashed towards him. "Blub!" said Schmink. They surrounded Fish. One hundred sea monsters around the evil man.

"AAARRRGGHH!" wailed Fish. It was over. He knew when he was beaten. He imagined that if Schminky said, "Blub," again the beasts would all jump on top of him. Attack him. He who until a few moments ago had been their master. The little critters!!

"Ok!" he said. "You win! I'll leave." Ronald Fish held his hands up and began to walk away.

Then he stopped and turned and said to Mr Parsnip, "They're only mops, you know. They're supposed to clean. That's what they're for."

To which Mr Parsnip replied, "Not any more they're not!"

Fish sloped away, off and out of the shopping centre and out of their lives. The Mops went "Blub!!" (which means "Yayyyyyy!!") They were gradually coming to their senses. Now that the nasty Fish who had enslaved them had gone they could think straight again. They could think about what they'd been through, the things he'd made them do. All that cleaning!! He'd even made them attack the children!!

Those children soon appeared, through the door that Fish had left open when he'd made his escape. They were a bit nervous of the Mops to start with but then Mr Parsnip explained what had happened.

The Mops very sadly said, "Blub," which Arnold explained meant, "Sorry, we didn't mean it," and they all hugged and made up.

Chapter 19. Normal.

While they'd been waiting in the car park, Sidney Brown had hopped back through the portal. He'd scuttled out of the staff room and over to the playing field, weaved his way through the crowd and reached the band as they were finishing.

"Mick," he panted, "Could you play a few more songs please? We're not ready to come back yet."

"Sure, Sid, no problems!" Mick Jagger replied.

That had bought them a bit of time. But the Stones couldn't play forever. Now the Mops had been rescued, the children would have to hurry back.

"Bye!" they all said, gave them one more hug and then zipped through the portal. They made it to the field as the parents were leaving.

"Where have you been?" Rudolph's father asked him.

"Playing," Rudolph replied. "The Rolling Stones is not my kind of music. I like Taylor Swift."

"Humph," the dad grunted. Taylor Swift!? Had he taught his son nothing?? The Rolling Stones – one of the best bands of all time – play a gig in Pinkerton and he – and the rest of Class 9 – decide they'd rather play some silly game instead. He would have to have stern words with his boy and possibly with Mr Parsnip as well. What was going on in Class 9, he often wondered. What were they being taught??

Nedrun walked home with her parents. They were talking away to each other about the Rolling Stones but she was thinking of her adventure – how they'd met the Mops in the first place, then Schminky had come home with them and they'd had such a lovely time, and then how they'd had to go back to Wales to rescue the Mops from evil Ronald Fish. What a tale!!! She doubted whether she'd sleep much that night, her mind was so alive! And even if she did sleep, her dreams would be full of the ocean and shopping centres and Mops. Lots and lots of Mops.

Parsnip, Schminky and Arnold stayed behind in North Wales for a while. They hopped on the magic skateboard and went to the beach. It was nice and quiet. No-one else was there apart from them.

"Blub," said Schminky to Arnold.

"Blub," Arnold replied.

Mr P understood that they were saying goodbye.

"Blub!" Arnold added, which meant, "I'll come and visit!"

"Blub," Schminky said, which meant, "that would be nice!"

They hugged for a long time then the beast dived into the deep blue sea and disappeared from sight. Arnold and Mr P waited for a moment alone on the beach. No more monsters. Just them. Humans. Mr P and Arnold Steenburgen. The rest of Class 9 with their parents back in Pinkerton.

Time to get back to normal.

Epilogue. Long John Hopscotch.

Schminky didn't swim back to their cave straightaway. He went in the opposite direction instead - on and on. If Mr Parsnip and Arnold could have seen him, they'd've wondered where he was going. But they couldn't so they didn't. And it didn't matter anyway cos Schminky knew where he was headed.

He was going to the pirate ship. The ship which had sunk two hundred years earlier and now lay on the ocean bed. The ship the golden watch had come from. The ship where the watch belonged.

Schminky swum right up to it. It looked old and broken but it was still glimmering with treasure scattered everywhere. Schminky wasn't interested in any of that though. No, he just wanted to return the watch to where it belonged. So he did. The Mop dropped the golden watch back into the shipwreck and then swam away to his cave.

The golden watch came to rest in the boat next to the skeleton of a pirate, Long John Hopscotch, the one who had owned it long ago. Its magical powers had helped him rule the seas and pile up millions of pounds of treasure.

Until he and all his crew had died in that terrible storm. What a shame! Poor Long John! Well, at least, he had his watch back now. It lay next to him, gleaming beautifully, beaming out magical power.

And, I don't know, it could be my imagination, but I think … the skeleton moved.

THE END

Printed in Great Britain
by Amazon